CITIES
HONG KONG

ABDO
Publishing Company

Nancy Furstinger

6/12

visit us at
www.abdopub.com

Published by ABDO Publishing Company, 4940 Viking Drive, Edina, Minnesota 55435.
Copyright © 2005 by Abdo Consulting Group, Inc. International copyrights reserved in all
countries. No part of this book may be reproduced in any form without written permission from
the publisher. The Checkerboard Library™ is a trademark and logo of ABDO Publishing Company.

Printed in the United States.

Cover Photo: Corbis
Interior Photos: Corbis pp. 1, 6-7, 11, 15, 16, 17, 21, 22, 23, 24, 27, 29; Getty Images pp. 9, 10, 13,
    14, 19, 25, 26, 28

Series Coordinator: Jennifer R. Krueger
Editors: Heidi M. Dahmes, Jennifer R. Krueger
Art Direction & Maps: Neil Klinepier

Library of Congress Cataloging-in-Publication Data

Furstinger, Nancy.
    Hong Kong / Nancy Furstinger.
        p. cm. -- (Cities)
    Includes index.
    Audience: 2-5.
    ISBN 1-59197-859-9
    1. Hong Kong (China)--Juvenile literature. I. Title.

DS796.H74F87 2005
951.25--dc22

                                                                2004056809

CONTENTS

HONG KONG

Hong Kong is located on the southeast coast of China. This special administrative region is on Hong Kong Island. But today, Hong Kong is made up of more than just Hong Kong Island. It contains more than 200 outlying islands and several regions.

Fishing villages dot some of these islands. However, most are deserted. Just north of Hong Kong Island is the Kowloon Peninsula. Farther north are the New Territories, which link the islands to mainland China. Together, Hong Kong Island and its surrounding regions span 424 square miles (1,098 sq km).

Hong Kong balances old and new, East and West. Here, tourists shop for cameras or for jade, which is a green gemstone. Skyscrapers battle mountains for space. Today, Hong Kong reigns as an international center of **culture** and trade.

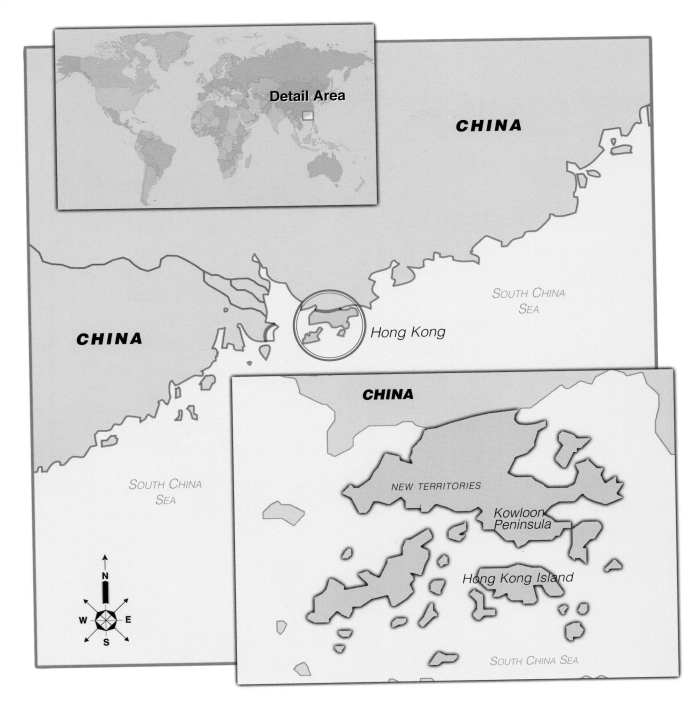

HONG KONG AT A GLANCE

Date of Founding: 1773

Population: 6,855,125

Metro Area: 31 square miles (80 sq km)

Average Temperatures:
- 61° Fahrenheit (16 °C) in cold season
- 84° Fahrenheit (29 °C) in warm season

Annual Rainfall: 85 inches (216 cm)

Elevation: 59 feet (18 m)

Landmark: The Peak

Money: Hong Kong Dollar

Languages: Cantonese, English

FUN FACTS

When eating in Hong Kong, never flip a fish over to reach the meat on the bottom. If someone does this, it is believed that the next fishing boat he or she passes will capsize. The proper method is to use chopsticks to break off pieces through the bones.

There are more cell phones per person in Hong Kong than in any other city in the world. About one in five Hong Kongers owns one.

Hong Kong is home to the world's largest neon sign. It is 365 feet (111 m) by 62 feet (19 m). The sign contains 8 miles (13 km) of tubing and weighs 88 tons (80 t).

TIMELINE

1773 - The British permanently settle the region of Hong Kong.

1839 - The first Opium War between China and Great Britain begins.

1842 - The first Opium War ends.

1856–1860 - The second Opium War is fought.

1941 - Japan attacks and occupies Hong Kong.

1945 - Japan surrenders; Great Britain regains control over Hong Kong.

1984 - China and Great Britain sign a joint declaration agreeing that Hong Kong will return to Chinese rule in 1997.

1997 - Hong Kong is returned to Chinese rule; Hong Kong's first chief executive is sworn into office.

OPIUM WARS

The earliest modern people settled in Hong Kong in the 1000s BC. In 100 BC, settlers from Canton, a major Chinese port northwest of Hong Kong, started coming to the area. But, major occupation did not occur for many years.

The area had a few small fishing villages. But, Hong Kong visitors did not stay long. Because of the small population, pirates were able to hide in the coves from authorities. Those hoping to honestly make fortunes had a bumpy route. That was because China restricted trade with Westerners.

The development of trade and settlement changed with the growing opium business. Opium is a drug made from poppy plants. Foreign dealers brought the drug to Hong Kong.

In AD 1773, the British discovered the value of the opium trade. The value of Hong Kong's natural harbor was also realized. So, the British decided to settle permanently in the region.

In 1839, China destroyed more than 20,000 chests of opium that the British were attempting to sell in China. Chinese

Opposite Page: *Even during the 1900s, security police guarded Hong Kong's harbors to stop drugs from being brought into the city.*

officials and opium traders clashed. The Chinese government's attempt to suppress the opium trade led to the first Opium War.

The first Opium War ended in 1842. Great Britain defeated China. China was forced to surrender Hong Kong to Britain. Under British rule, the opium trade continued on Hong Kong Island.

Opium influenced Hong Kong's politics for many decades. The second Opium War was fought between 1856 and 1860. China lost and handed the Kowloon Peninsula over to the British Empire. The New Territories followed in 1898. A lease ensured that Great Britain would rule the land for 99 years.

In 1941, Japan attacked and occupied Hong Kong. During the Japanese occupation, Hong Kong's population dropped. In 1945, the Japanese surrendered and the British regained control of Hong Kong.

A victory parade wound through the streets of Hong Kong Island to celebrate the Japanese surrender.

Hong Kong boasts some of the world's tallest buildings.

In 1976, the Chinese ruler Mao Tse-tung died. The new Chinese government worked to return Hong Kong to Chinese rule. In 1984, Britain and China signed a joint declaration. With this, Britain agreed to return Hong Kong to China in 1997.

CHINESE RULE

Great Britain's lease on Hong Kong expired on July 1, 1997. At that time, Hong Kong returned to Chinese rule. For the next 50 years, the city will be a special administrative region of the People's Republic of China.

China controls Hong Kong's military and foreign policies. But, Hong Kong manages its own **economy**. It also has limited **democracy**.

A chief executive heads the new Hong Kong government. The first chief executive was chosen by a 400-member selection committee that had been picked by China's government. The group selected Tung Chee-hwa. He was sworn in on July 1, 1997, for a five-year term.

Like the land he governs, Tung's life blends East and West. He was born in Shanghai, China, and moved to Hong Kong in 1947. Tung was educated in Britain and worked in the United States for six years.

Tung Chee-hwa

Despite his background, Tung has had two difficult terms. Hong Kong suffered a recession in 1998 after the Asian financial crisis. And in 2003, Tung was criticized for his slow response to a Severe Acute Respiratory Syndrome (SARS) outbreak that led to many deaths.

TRANSPORTATION

Hong Kong is small and crowded. The roads are clogged, and vehicles drive on the left-hand side of the road! But, it has a modern, efficient public transportation system.

Many Hong Kongers use public transportation such as buses, **trams**, and ferries. Another form of public transportation is the rickshaw. Men pull their passengers in these chairs on wheels. This form of transportation was brought to Hong Kong in 1870.

Today, the rickshaw tradition is racing to a halt. Some city dwellers feel that the sight of rickshaw pullers is shameful. No

These double-decker trams are a popular form of transportation in Hong Kong.

licenses are being renewed. The few rickshaw pullers left depend on tourists to survive.

For getting to and from Hong Kong, vehicle and subway tunnels link the island with the Kowloon Peninsula. From there, roads and an electric railroad provide access by land to China.

Hong Kong also has two international airports. By sea, ships enter through Kwai Chung, one of Hong Kong's container ports. Most of the trade that travels over the seas passes through this busy port.

The Kwai Chung container port

TRADE GATEWAY

Hong Kong has grown into a major port. While workers in London and New York sleep, Hong Kong is the center of world trade. It is also a gateway for trade with mainland China.

The city itself has few natural resources. However, it makes up for this with eager workers. They process and assemble goods from raw materials **imported** from other countries. Some of Hong Kong's

Workers at an assembly line in a Hong Kong factory

many **exports** are **textiles**, watches, electronics, and printed materials.

Local produce is also in short supply. Farmland on the island is vanishing. Hong Kong must import most of its food.

A worker picks leaves in a rice paddy field.

China is the main source for food **imports**. However, Hong Kong's fishing industry is well developed and keeps the **economy** afloat. So do tourists.

Tourism is one of Hong Kong's biggest industries. Hong Kong is a duty-free port. So, shopping is Hong Kong's main draw. People search for Chinese arts and **antiques** on Hollywood Road. Movies are also made in the city. It makes more feature films than any other place in the world.

CLIMATE

Hong Kong's weather is affected by the South China Sea and the North Pacific Ocean. **Monsoons** from the southwest bring hot and humid weather in the summer. During this time, many visitors enjoy Hong Kong's spectacular beaches. Repulse Bay is the most popular.

From May to September is the rainy season. About 80 percent of Hong Kong's rain falls during these months. September is the most common month for uncertain weather. Hong Kongers are likely to see weather ranging from a tropical storm to a typhoon.

Cold winds blow in from the northern Asian landmass in winter. Winter stretches from October to late January or early February. This is the best time to visit the region because it is cooler.

Opposite Page: *A typhoon is a severe tropical hurricane. During a severe typhoon in Hong Kong, winds can reach speeds of nearly 140 miles per hour (225 km/h). Hong Kongers cannot go outside and many businesses shut down.*

HONG KONGERS

Hong Kong has one of the world's highest densities of people. Ninety percent of Hong Kong's residents live on just 15 percent of the land. This is due to Hong Kong's steep **terrain**.

The official languages of Hong Kong are English and a Cantonese dialect of Chinese. About 97 percent of city residents are Chinese. But, many **immigrant** groups also make up the population of Hong Kong. The largest immigrant group is Filipino.

Some of Hong Kong's immigrants moved to escape wars and **rebellions**. Others fled China and arrived on the island illegally. The **Communist** Party's victory in mainland China in 1949 led many to escape to Hong Kong.

Then in the 1990s, thousands of educated professionals fled Hong Kong. They feared that the Chinese government would try to control Hong Kong too tightly. In 1990, about 1,000 people per week moved to the United States, Canada, and Australia.

By 1990, Hong Kong was home to more than 56,000 Vietnamese. In 1991, a program was started to return these families to Vietnam.

Such a diverse population brings many religions to Hong Kong, as well. **Buddhists** and **Taoists** make up 90 percent of the population.

Many different people have ruled Hong Kong. The British influence is still seen in Hong Kong's education system. And, most schools provide instruction in Chinese, with English as a second language.

Hong Kong offers three years of voluntary kindergarten education. Kindergarten education is followed by six years of required, free primary schooling. Students then spend five years in secondary education.

Primary education classes include social studies and music.

Higher education is very competitive. There is limited space at the local universities. The oldest and most difficult to gain entrance to is the University of Hong Kong. This school was founded in 1911.

Food and the eating of it are taken just as seriously as education. Hong Kong food is Chinese food. Meals are noisy, social events. Dishes are ordered and shared with a group.

Rice is a part of every meal. The main dishes are fresh, simply prepared seafood and fish. Pork, chicken, duck, and beef are also popular.

Cantonese cuisine

Dishes are often served with different sauces, such as soy sauce, hot mustard, or chili sauce.

Cantonese cuisine is the most popular in Hong Kong. Fresh ingredients are very important in Cantonese cooking. Some expensive dishes include abalone, shark's fin, and bird's nest. Roasted pigeon is a Cantonese specialty.

Cantonese cuisine

CHINESE CUSTOMS

Hong Kongers have adopted many Chinese customs. One that continues today is yum cha, which means "drinking tea." Chinese tea is an important part of Hong Kong culture. When tea drinkers tap the table with three fingers of the same hand, it is a silent expression of gratitude to the person who filled their cup.

The Chinese believe that foods have healing powers. Some Chinese practice jinbu. This includes eating special foods and herbs that are supposed to improve vision and strength. Chinese medicine is also very popular in Hong Kong. This medicine treats the whole body instead of just the illness.

Chinese New Year parade participants

The Chinese New Year is the most important holiday in Hong Kong. It is based on the lunar calendar, which traces the phases of the moon.

Hong Kongers celebrate the New Year with a three-day holiday. During the festivities, fireworks explode over Victoria Harbor. An international parade snakes through the city. People bang drums and perform lion dances.

People also visit an ancient banyan tree called the Wishing Tree during the Chinese New Year. They write wishes on incense papers and throw them into the air. The wish will be granted if the paper snags on the tree's branches.

Lanterns star in the Mid-Autumn Festival. They are carried to special spots such as mountains and beaches. Here, people can gaze at the harvest moon.

People can't see the ghostly spirits honored during the Bun Festival on Cheung Chau Island. This is a weeklong, lively celebration. The last event

used to include young people who climbed bamboo bun towers. However, this ritual ended in 1978 when a tower collapsed.

Hovering souls are the focus during the Hungry Ghost Festival. Ghosts roam the earth. And, people burn money and other offerings to calm the spirits.

When not going to festivals, many Hong Kongers enjoy exercising. Many practice Tai Chi, a Chinese form of unarmed combat. Each morning in Hong Kong parks, people perform these slow movements. Tai Chi exercises the mind, soul, and body.

Kung fu, which means "skill," is another **martial art**. Kung fu serves as both an exercise and a form of

People burn their offerings during the Hungry Ghost Festival.

Children enjoy kung fu, too.

personal combat. As a **martial art**, kung fu dates back to the 1100s BC. Performed as exercise, it resembles Tai Chi.

Hearts beat faster during the Hong Kong Sevens. This three-day rugby event attracts fans to Hong Kong Stadium. Crowds in wild costumes pack the arena. Twenty-four teams from around the world compete. Seven players on each rugby team play a fast-paced game. The action on the field is nonstop.

ATTRACTIONS

Visitors take in the sights of Hong Kong from a restaurant on the Peak.

Tourists and Hong Kong residents love to visit the Peak. This central peak rises 1,825 feet (556 m). Visitors ride the Peak **Tram** up into the clouds. In seven minutes, the tram delivers riders to the summit. There, they enjoy the view.

During their leisure time, Hong Kongers have many different opportunities to view animals in their natural environments. Striped and spotted creatures prowl at the Hong Kong Zoological and Botanical Gardens. This zoo opened in AD 1864 and features many animals and plants.

Birds flock to the Mai Po Nature Reserve. Here, visitors have sighted more than 340 kinds of birds. The mangrove forests host endangered species such as the black-faced

spoonbill. Only 1,000 live in the world.

During migration, birds seek out the safe haven at Mai Po. They arrive from China, Mongolia, and Siberia. At Mai Po they rest, feed, and boost their energy for their next journey.

Hong Kong is famous for more than 600 temples. These are usually **Buddhist** or **Taoist**. Or they honor Confucius, a philosopher from the 500s BC. The Temple of Ten Thousand Buddhas is reached by climbing more than 400 stairs. Here, 12,800 tiny Buddha statues are stacked to the ceiling.

GLOSSARY

antique - an old item that has collectible value.

Buddhism - a religion founded in India by Siddhartha Gautama. It teaches that pain and evil are caused by desire. If people have no desire, they will achieve a state of happiness called Nirvana.

Communism - a social and economic system in which everything is owned by the government and given to the people as needed.

culture - the customs, arts, and tools of a nation or people at a certain time.

democracy - a governmental system in which the people vote on how to run their country.

economy - the way a nation uses its money, goods, and natural resources.

export - to send goods to another country for sale or trade.

immigrate - to enter another country to live. A person who immigrates is called an immigrant.

import - to bring in goods from another country for sale or trade.

martial art - a sport practiced for combat or self-defense.

monsoon - a season of wind that sometimes brings heavy rain.

rebellion - an armed resistance or defiance of a government.

Taoism - a religion that emphasizes harmony with nature and people.

terrain - the physical features of an area of land. Mountains, rivers, and canyons can all be part of a terrain.

textile - of or having to do with the designing, manufacturing, or producing of woven fabric.

tram - a carrier that travels on rails or an overhead cable.

Confucius - kuhn-FYOO-shuhs
Mao Tse-tung - MOWD-ZUH-DUHNG
Tai Chi - TEYE JEE
Taoism - DOW-ih-zuhm

To learn more about Hong Kong, visit ABDO Publishing Company on the World Wide Web at **www.abdopub.com**. Web sites about Hong Kong are featured on our Book Links page. These links are routinely monitored and updated to provide the most current information available.

INDEX

A
attractions 18, 24, 25, 26, 27, 28, 29
Australia 20

C
Canada 20
China 4, 8, 10, 11, 12, 15, 16, 17, 20, 23, 26, 29
climate 18
Confucius 29

E
economy 4, 8, 10, 12, 13, 15, 16, 17
education 22, 23

F
festivals 24, 25, 26
food 16, 17, 23

G
government 12
Great Britain 8, 10, 11, 12, 16, 22

I
immigrants 20

J
Japan 10

K
Kwai Chung 15

L
language 20, 22

M
Mao Tse-tung 11
Mongolia 29

O
Opium Wars 8, 10

P
Pacific Ocean 18

R
religion 22, 29

S
Siberia 29
South China Sea 18
sports 26, 27

T
transportation 14, 15
Tung Chee-hwa 12, 13

U
United States 12, 16, 20